FATHER'S
RUBBER SHOES

by Yumi Heo

ORCHARD BOOKS/NEW YORK

Orchard Books
95 Madison Avenue
New York, NY 10016

Manufactured in the United States of America
Printed by Barton Press, Inc.
Bound by Horowitz/Rae
Book design by Rosanne Kakos-Main

10 9 8 7 6 5 4 3 2 1

The text of this book is set in 17 point ITC Clearface.
The illustrations are oil paint, pencil, and collage
reproduced in full color.

Library of Congress Cataloging-in-Publication Data

Heo, Yumi.
Father's rubber shoes / by Yumi Heo.
    p. cm.
Summary: Yungsu misses Korea terribly until he begins
to make friends in America.
ISBN 0-531-06873-0. —ISBN 0-531-08723-9 (lib. bdg.)
[1. Korean Americans—Fiction. 2. Homesickness—Fiction.
3. Friendship—Fiction.] I. Title.
PZ7.H4117Fat   1995
[E]—dc20   94-21961

For my brothers,
Yun and Yunsu

Yungsu walked down the street toward the playground. He put his hands in his pockets and kicked an empty can. It was Saturday. Hand in hand, families were going in and out of stores.

Yungsu gazed through the window of his father's store. His father's hands were moving quickly from the cash register to the groceries on the counter to the hands of his customers.

Yungsu kept walking down the street.

No one Yungsu knew was at the playground. He sat on the swing and thought of his friends in Korea. Yungsu missed them very much.

During supper, Yungsu's mother noticed that he was very quiet. She asked him what was wrong.

Yungsu hesitated and then blurted out, "Since we moved to America, Father doesn't have any time to play with me and he doesn't smile anymore. Nobody plays with me.
"Can we go back to Korea? Mom!"
Yungsu's mother looked thoughtful.

That night, Yungsu dreamed of playing horse
with his friends in Korea.

Something woke him up. It was his father's rough hands holding Yungsu's small ones. Yungsu's father had come to see Yungsu sleeping, as he always did when he came home from the store.

"When I was a child," Yungsu's father said, "I wore straw shoes. Then one birthday, my mother bought me a pair of rubber shoes. I was so happy. In those days, rubber shoes were the best shoes to own. Very few people had them.

"I loved them and wanted to keep them a long, long time. When I walked alone, I took them off and carried them in my hands.

"If I saw somebody coming, I put them on."

His father paused. "I want to give you something—like my rubber shoes, but something you can have all the time. That's why we're here. I hope you understand."

Yungsu blinked his eyes.

"Sweet dreams, son," Yungsu's father said, tucking him in.

The next morning, Yungsu's mother told Yungsu
she was cooking *bulgogi* for lunch. *Bulgogi!* That
was Yungsu's favorite food. Thinly sliced meat in a
sweet soy sauce. Just thinking about it made his
mouth water. Yungsu helped his mother clean the
red-tipped lettuce and set the table.

Then he wrapped a *bulgogi* with rice in the lettuce and popped it into his mouth. He could not close his mouth. It even puffed out his cheeks.

"Mom! I will take some *bulgogi* to Dad at the store," Yungsu announced after he swallowed.

Yungsu's mother smiled. "Your father would love it." She put the *bulgogi* in a lunch box.

Yungsu walked down the street. On the way he met Alex, from his school.

"What are you carrying?" Alex asked. "It smells good."

"It's a Korean food, *bulgogi*. Here, try some." Yungsu opened the lunch box and gave a piece of *bulgogi* to Alex.

"Wow! It's delicious," Alex said, licking his lips.

"Want to come over to my house for lunch next weekend? I'll ask my mom to make it for us."

"Great—I can't wait!" Alex kept licking his lips.

When Yungsu crossed the street, he saw the fruits outside his father's store—oranges, grapes, bananas, and apples—all cleaned by his father's hands. They were lined up neatly and seemed to smile.